THE STALLION
OF BOX CANYON

TREASURED HORSES COLLECTION™

titles in Large-Print Editions:

THE
STALLION OF
BOX CANYON

*The story of a wild Mustang and
the girl who wins his trust*

Written by **Jahnna N. Malcolm**
Illustrated by **Sandy Rabinowitz**
Cover Illustration by **Christa Keiffer**
Developed by Nancy Hall, Inc.

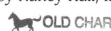
Gareth Stevens Publishing
MILWAUKEE

For a free color catalog describing Gareth Stevens' list of high-quality books and multimedia programs, call 1-800-542-2595 (USA) or 1-800-461-9120 (Canada). Gareth Stevens Publishing's Fax: (414) 225-0377.

Library of Congress Cataloging-in-Publication Data

Malcolm, Jahnna N.
The stallion of Box Canyon / written by Jahnna N. Malcolm; illustrated by Sandy Rabinowitz; cover illustration by Christa Keiffer.
p. cm.
Originally published: Dyersville, Iowa: Ertl Co., 1997.
(Treasured horses collection)
Summary: Convinced that she is wanted only as a servant in her new home with relatives on a Wyoming ranch, orphaned, eleven-year-old Abby is unhappy until she finds and befriends an injured Mustang and determines to try to save it no matter what the cost is to herself.
ISBN 0-8368-2283-8 (lib. bdg.)
[1. Orphans—Fiction. 2. Ranch life—Wyoming—Fiction. 3. Mustang—Fiction. 4. Horses—Fiction. 5. Wyoming—Fiction.]
I. Rabinowitz, Sandy, ill. II. Title. III. Series: Treasured horses collection.
PZ7.M2897St 1999
[Fic]—dc21   98-44734

This edition first published in 1999 by
Gareth Stevens Publishing
1555 North RiverCenter Drive, Suite 201
Milwaukee, Wisconsin 53212 USA

© 1997 by Nancy Hall, Inc.
First published by The ERTL Company, Inc., Dyersville, Iowa.

Treasured Horses Collection is a registered trademark of The ERTL Company, Inc.

Printed in the United States of America

1 2 3 4 5 6 7 8 9 03 02 01 00 99

CONTENTS

CHAPTER
ONE

Abby the Orphan

Abigail Armstrong watched the huge black steam engine pull into the station, and her knees went weak. In a few minutes, she would be on that train, saying good-bye to Davenport, Iowa, and heading out for the Territory of Wyoming.

"Say, ain't that Abby Armstrong?" a scruffy boy in patched wool pants and yellowing cotton shirt called from the door of the depot.

Abby didn't need to look. She knew who it was. Thirteen-year-old Budge Jenkins, the town bully. Next to Budge stood her cousin, Luke, a gaunt boy of fourteen.

"Yep. That's Abby, all right. Pa's shipping her off today," Luke explained in his irritatingly nasal voice.

Abby could feel her cheeks heat up as the two boys discussed her. She clutched her small canvas bag with all of her belongings close to her chest and tilted her chin up defiantly.

"You'd think an orphan like her would be grateful your Pa took her in," Budge said, moving across the train platform toward Abby.

"Them's Pa's words exactly," Luke replied, keeping in step with Budge. "But she's pig-headed. Refused to wear the clothes my sisters give her. Wouldn't help Ma with the chores. Spent all day climbing trees in the apple orchard."

"Whoo-ee!" Budge whistled. "That musta made your ma mad."

"Madder than a cat caught in a briar patch. 'Course Ma never liked Abby's parents. They thought they was better'n all of us, just cause Abby's Pa was a newspaper man. Well, look what happened to 'em."

"What?" Budge asked.

"Diphtheria. Took Aunt Emily, Uncle Will, and the baby, just like that." Luke snapped his fingers. "They was dead in seven days."

Budge snorted. "I guess that showed 'em!"

Abby dropped her canvas bag and spun to face the two boys. Her green eyes flashed angrily, and her tangled yellow hair whipped across her face.

"Lucas Armstrong and Budge Jenkins, you shut your mouths!" she shouted. "My mama and papa were great people. They had more smarts in their little fingers than you two have in your entire bodies. And if you say one more bad word about them, I swear I'll . . . I'll . . ."

"You'll what?" Budge asked, shoving his pimply face close to hers.

Even though Abby was small for an eleven-year-old, she was tough. She had to be. After a year of being passed from one household to another, she had developed a very thick skin. And hard knuckles.

"I'll clobber you," she whispered directly into Budge's face. And she meant it!

Budge's eyes widened, and he took a step backwards, bumping into Luke. "That girl's a wildcat!" he sputtered.

Luke backed up, too. "That's why they're shipping her off to the Wild West. It's the only place left that'll take her!"

Abby's face was now a blazing crimson color. She raised one fist and was just about to sock Luke in the nose, when a man from the Rock Island Railroad stepped out of the depot.

"Will all of the orphans line up by the luggage car?" he called. "All of you from the Children's Aid

Society and the Juvenile Asylum, line up over there."

Luke grinned. "That's you, Abigail."

Abby was indignant. "It most certainly is not! I don't know any of those children!"

But the conductor thought differently. He spied the tag pinned to Abby's shabby dress.

"You there." He squinted one eye to read the words on her tag out loud. "Number 52. Bound for Laramie. Line up with the others."

"But I'm not one of them!" Abby knew very well who those *others* were. They were part of the Orphan Train system that took abandoned children off the streets of New York and Boston and shipped them west. She had *not* been abandoned! Her parents had died.

"All children traveling alone, move over there!" The conductor pointed impatiently at a group of children huddled together by the luggage car. All of them wore tags, and all looked worn out from their trip from the East.

Abby wasn't about to ride in the luggage car. She glared at the conductor and barked, "I won't!"

"Oh, yes, you will," a woman's voice trilled from beside Abby. It was her Aunt Esther. She gripped Abby by the arm and squeezed tightly. "You'll do whatever that good man says."

"Ow!" Abby tried to wrench her arm loose. "That hurts!"

Aunt Esther and her best friend, Mrs. Hickman, had come to the station to make sure Abby got on the train. They looked like two plump partridges in their best "go-to-meeting" clothes and feathered hats.

Aunt Esther dragged Abby to the group of children clustered around the luggage car, handed Abby her ticket, and barked, "Now stay put!"

Then Aunt Esther stepped back to join Mrs. Hickman. She pulled a handkerchief out of the base of her sleeve and dabbed dramatically at the corners of her eyes.

"Now don't you start feeling bad, Esther," Mrs. Hickman clucked, patting her on the arm. "Your house was overcrowded, and this child was just another mouth to feed." She pursed her lips and added, "You did your best, Esther, no one can say otherwise."

"When her ma and pa passed away," Aunt Esther explained, "I knew we had to take her in. It was the right thing to do."

"And you did just that," Mrs. Hickman reminded her. "And don't forget, you weren't the only one to have trouble with her. Remember the Lloyd family in Ames? They took her into their home, and what did she do? Run away."

Aunt Esther nodded grimly. "Impossible. That's the word they used to describe her. *Im*-possible."

Abby remembered the Lloyds. They *did* take her in. But only because they wanted to loot her family's home. They took the piano, her mother's walnut china cupboard and dining set, her father's books and clothes, and almost every piece of jewelry that her mother owned.

The one thing they didn't get was the necklace Abby's mother was wearing when she died. It was an odd pendant—half a heart, strung on a gold chain—but it was her mother's favorite.

Abby patted her canvas suitcase. The necklace, along with the blue ribbons from her brother's booties and a tintype of her father, were inside. Those few treasures were all that Abby had left of her family as she headed off to live with her mother's sister, Mary, on a ranch.

While Aunt Esther and Mrs. Hickman gossiped and the train was readied for departure, Abby hopped onto the edge of the wooden luggage cart and waited with the other orphan children.

She still didn't feel she was one of them. She knew who her parents were. Just to reassure herself, Abby felt in her bag once again for her treasures. Her hand touched the cool frame of the tintype.

She pulled it out and, carefully balancing it in her lap, stared down at the picture. It had been taken on her tenth birthday. Her father, a handsome man with dark brown eyes and a fine moustache, held the reins of a shaggy-maned pony. Astride the pony was a pretty little girl with sausage curls and two big bows

in her hair, and a grin that stretched from ear to ear.

Abby smiled. That had been a wonderful birthday. Her parents had surprised her with a brown–and–white pinto named Toby. Even her baby brother, Benjamin, had joined in the celebration by burying his face in the cherry pie her mother had baked for the occasion.

Abby's smile slowly faded. It was barely a month after her birthday party that the sickness came.

Little Ben was the first to go. Then Papa. And last, Mama. She lay in bed, burning with fever and gasping for breath for two nights and days. Then it was over. Abby's entire family—wiped out in a week.

Abby squinted up at the white puffs of smoke spewing from the train's engine, trying to remember if she'd ever been happy since.

Whoo-oo!

The train whistle blew its lonesome call, and Abby leapt to her feet. She joined the line of orphans waiting to climb up the steps into the train.

To her relief, she discovered the children didn't have to ride in the luggage car, after all. They were in a real passenger car with windows. It wasn't as fancy as the Pullman cars near the rear of the train, but at least it had seats. Flat wooden benches lined either side of the aisle.

Abby found a place by the window near the back of the car, hoping to catch Aunt Esther's eye so she could wave good-bye. But her aunt was too busy gossiping with Mrs. Hickman to notice Abby had left the platform.

"All aboard!" the conductor called.

Aunt Esther looked up in surprise and searched the windows for Abby.

Abby pressed her hand against the glass, but Aunt Esther didn't see her.

With a jerk and a hiss of brakes the train rolled forward. As the train chugged out of the station, Abby watched the figures of her aunt and Mrs. Hickman slide by the window. "Good-bye, Iowa," Abby whispered.

The rhythm of the wheels quickened as the train gathered speed.

One of the kids across the aisle cupped his hands around his mouth and announced, "Next stop, the wild, Wild West!"

Westward Ho!

Abby wiped a grimy smudge off her cheek and stared out the stagecoach window.

Days of constant jostling on the hard wooden benches of the Rock Island and Union Pacific railroads had worn her out. The trains ran in a straight line across treeless plains, then pierced a spine of rugged mountains into the Wyoming Territory.

At Laramie she had been put on a stagecoach that bounced north along the edge of the Laramie River.

A balding circuit preacher sat across from Abby, speaking to the young woman beside him. She was

to be the new school marm in Rock River. Abby
sensed that the woman felt as frightened and alone
as she did.

Beside Abby sat a heavy man with a red face and
thick jowls. He chewed tobacco, and every so often he
spat a thin stream of brown juice into a tin cup. Abby
tried to lean as far away from him as possible.

The Laramie River wound through the valley in
great undulating curves. On the horizon huge, craggy
mountains towered above the valley floor, their snowy
peaks shrouded in thick white clouds.

"So wild and beautiful!" Abby whispered.

At the same time a tiny voice inside her warned,
Don't get too attached. Every time you do, it gets
taken away from you.

When the stagecoach finally rumbled into
Medicine Bow, Abby sat up in her seat, peering
anxiously out the window. She was covered from
head to toe in black soot and red dust from the long
journey. Her mouth was dry and gritty, and every
muscle in her body ached. But still she was excited.

This little town, which consisted of one rickety
wooden building and a few tents, would be her new
home.

Abby spied a family standing in front of the
wooden building. The man was tall and handsome.

He wore blue Union pants with a broad yellow stripe down the sides, a vest over his collarless white shirt, and tooled leather boots that stretched to his knees. Around his neck was a bright blue bandanna.

Beside him stood a blonde woman in a twill skirt, gingham blouse, broad-brimmed leather hat, and boots just like the man's. A round-faced girl with brown braids in a cotton print shirtdress was hopping up and down next to the couple.

"That must be them!" Abby whispered. "Captain Joe, Aunt Mary, and Cousin Elizabeth."

All three of them were grinning and waving merrily. They looked genuinely happy to see her.

Abby would have loved to jump down from the coach and leap right into Aunt Mary's open arms. But that little voice—the one deep inside her—said, Don't do it. You can't trust them. You can't trust anybody.

Instead, Abby stood stiffly by the coach as the family rushed over to greet her.

"Oh, Abigail!" Aunt Mary cried, scooping her up in her arms and hugging her tight. "Am I glad to see you! I've dreamed about this day." Aunt Mary's voice caught in her throat as tears streamed down her cheeks. "Forgive me, honey," she whispered. "You look so much like your mother, it's almost too much to bear."

"Let me hug my cousin!" Elizabeth cried. "It's my turn." She spun Abby around to face her.

Although Elizabeth was the same age as Abby, she was two full inches taller. She had warm, brown eyes, freckles that dotted her tanned cheeks, and a big friendly smile. Her hug nearly took Abby's breath away.

"I'm so excited I could spit," Elizabeth said. "Mama and I fixed up a bed for you in my room. We put a quilt on it that my mama and your mama stitched when they were little girls."

Abby's heart leapt up. How wonderful! Something still remained that her mother had touched, other than the gold necklace with the broken heart.

Captain Joe was the last to greet her. He took off his hat and smiled warmly at her. Abby gazed up at him in wonder. She didn't think she'd ever seen such a handsome moustache. It was waxed and curled up into a perfect handlebar. His face was deeply tanned, which made his blue eyes look even brighter.

"Welcome to Wyoming, Abigail," Captain Joe rumbled in a voice so deep Abby could almost feel the ground vibrate beneath her boots. "The Carter family is pleased to have you join us at the Double Diamond Ranch."

As the family led her to the buckboard wagon

that would carry them out to the ranch, she glanced back over her shoulder at the stagecoach.

Don't get too comfortable, the little voice inside her warned. It won't be long before you're back on that stagecoach.

The Double Diamond

D*ing-a-ling-a-ling!*

The clang of the cook's triangle shattered the morning stillness, and Abby sat up in her bed with a start.

Sunlight poured through the bedroom window onto the patchwork quilt covering her bed. She quickly checked the other bed to see if her cousin Elizabeth was still asleep.

Elizabeth was gone. Her bed was made, and her nightgown was neatly folded and placed on top of her pillow.

"What time is it?" Abby said out loud, rubbing the sleep from her eyes.

Elizabeth ducked her head into the room. "Time to get up, sleepyhead. Cook's got breakfast on the table, and he sure gets riled if the food gets cold."

Abby threw back the covers and looked down at herself. She was wearing a pretty white muslin nightgown with lace at the cuffs. "Where did I get this?"

"It used to be one of mine," Elizabeth explained. "I'm happy it fits you."

"Oh," Abby mumbled. After her arrival at the ranch the night before, she'd taken a hot bath in a washtub in the kitchen, nibbled on a sourdough biscuit, and collapsed into bed. She couldn't even

24

remember putting on the nightgown.

"So what do you think of our room?" Elizabeth asked, gesturing to the jar of wildflowers she'd placed on the knotty pine dresser that stood across from their beds.

Abby blinked several times as she looked around the room. It was a cheery place, with whitewashed walls and polished wooden floorboards. The dresser, bedsteads, and chair were rough-hewn. But there were accents everywhere of things that clearly came from back east.

Four gilt-framed colored illustrations of birds hung on the wall. A lace doily was draped over the simple wooden table between their beds. And several postcards of scenes from Chicago framed the mirror above the dresser.

Abby loved it, but she couldn't bring herself to tell Elizabeth that. She just shrugged and said, "It's fine, I guess."

Elizabeth sat on the bed across from Abby. "I was afraid you wouldn't like it. That you'd be homesick."

"Homesick?" Abby cocked her head. "For what?"

The last three places she'd stayed, Abby had either slept on the floor in a borrowed blanket or been forced to curl up at the end of someone's bed. How could she be homesick for that?

"For, um, your own room," Elizabeth stammered. "You know, with Aunt Emily and Uncle—"

Abby cut her cousin off with a sharp wave of her hand. "That was long ago," she said stiffly. "I barely remember it."

"Oh." Elizabeth stood up awkwardly. "Well, I guess I'll let you get dressed. Hurry and join us for breakfast. After we eat, I'll show you around the ranch."

Abby took her time getting dressed. She didn't want to appear too eager to please. She knew from experience that as soon as she acted like she really wanted something, it was taken away from her.

By the time she made an appearance in the dining room, the table was deserted. A single plate with silverware and a glass were all that remained on the table.

Aunt Mary swept in from the kitchen, a long white apron over her red-and-white gingham smock. "There you are!" she greeted Abby. "We were afraid you were going to skip breakfast altogether."

"No, ma'am," Abby said. "I had some trouble finding my clothes."

Aunt Mary's hand flew to her mouth. "Oh, I'm sorry. While you were asleep, I took your traveling clothes to wash them. I forgot to have Elizabeth tell you that I'd left another set of clothes for you on the chair." She gestured at Abby's navy blue-and-white polka dot dress, with matching blue cotton leggings and leather boots, and smiled. "But I see you found them. Do they fit?"

Abby nodded. "Yes, ma'am." Not only did they fit perfectly—they were almost like new. Something she hadn't experienced in a long time. But she didn't tell Aunt Mary that.

Aunt Mary studied Abby's face. Finally she said, "Well, let's get some food in you. Take a seat."

Breakfast was delicious: a plate of steaming hotcakes with huckleberry syrup, three strips of bacon, and a big glass of milk.

"Elizabeth wants to show you around the ranch," Aunt Mary said, as she cleared Abby's plate. "She's in the henhouse, gathering eggs. Why don't you join her?"

Abby stepped onto the front porch of the family ranch house, expecting to find the chicken coop right outside. But she was surprised to discover that the Double Diamond Ranch was far larger than any farm she had ever seen in Iowa.

Open range stretched eastward as far as the eye could see. The prairie was dotted with clusters of cattle. Surrounding the western side of the range were huge red cliffs. They looked like a layer cake.

The ranch house was a rambling two-story

building made of smooth ponderosa pine logs that were each at least a foot thick. The smaller outbuildings looked like echoes of the main house, each a little log cabin with its own cedar shake or sod roof.

"Hey, lil' lady, you look lost!" a voice drawled from behind her.

Abby spun around. Standing before her was a scrawny, bowlegged man dressed in woolly chaps, pointed boots, and a huge hat with a broad brim. His face looked like wrinkled leather. And when he grinned, Abby saw that he only had one front tooth.

"I'm looking for the place where you keep chickens," she explained.

The man squinted one eye shut. "You must be that little girl come from back east."

Abby tilted up her chin. "I'm Abigail Armstrong. But most folks call me Abby."

"That suits me just fine, Miss Abby." The little man tipped his hat toward her. "Pleased to meet you. I'm Big Tim. And I believe I saw Miss Elizabeth out by the henhouse. Which would be that-a-way." Big Tim gestured to a small shed with a sloping roof about a hundred yard to Abby's right.

Abby hesitated. She didn't know if she was ready to be with Elizabeth, just yet. She wanted to investigate her new surroundings by herself first.

"What's that over there?" Abby pointed to a fenced-in area in the distance. A green swath of pasture spread out from beneath the fence poles and rails until it met a flowing stream lined with cottonwoods and weeping willows.

"That's the horse corral," Big Tim explained. "And to the north there is the cookshack, bunkhouse, blacksmith shop, and storage sheds."

A wisp of smoke puffed out of the stovepipe of the cookshack's sod roof. Abby decided to start her exploration there.

She bid farewell to Big Tim and hurried toward the little log hut. Along the way, she bumped into the ranch foreman, Waddy Hancock.

Waddy was just the opposite of Big Tim. He was huge—tall, barrel-chested, with a red beard that exploded out of his chin in all directions.

"I take it you're Miss Abby," Waddy declared, tipping his low-crowned hat, which had a brim even wider than Big Tim's. "Welcome to the Double Diamond."

Waddy clapped his hat back on his head and sauntered off toward the barn. With each long stride, his leather chaps flapped and spurs jingled.

Then a boy about the same age as Abby's cousin Luke trotted by on a black-and-white pinto. His chaps were streaked with trail dust, and so was the big yellow bandanna draped over his plaid shirt. "Name's Curly," the boy called out as he passed by.

"Nice to meet you," she said. "I'm Abby."

"I know. Missed you at breakfast."

Abby turned in a circle as she watched Curly lope toward the horse corral. "Sorry," she called. "I guess I overslept."

When she poked her head in the open doorway of the cookshack, she was instantly hit with the savory aroma of bubbling stew.

Then a terrifying voice roared, "Who dares enter my domain without knocking?"

CHAPTER FOUR

Just-Me-Abigail

"**I**t's just me, Abigail," Abby cried, quickly stepping back outside.

"Just-Me-Abigail?" A tall black man loomed in the doorway, clutching a long wooden ladle in his right hand and a cast-iron pot lid in his left. He was dressed like a cowboy except, instead of chaps, he wore an apron around his waist. "What kind of tom-fool name is that for a person?"

"I just wondered who lived here. So I peeked inside," she quickly explained. "I didn't mean to trespass, or anything."

The cook had a long thin face. A bowler perched on the top of his head. He stared at Abby with his dark eyes for quite awhile. She held her breath, not knowing whether to run or stay.

"Well, Just-Me-Abigail, I'm making up a mess of Anything'll-Do-Stew." His mouth creased into a grin. "Care to have a taste?"

Abby wasn't too sure. With a name like Anything'll-Do, the stew sounded like it could be made out of lizard and frog guts. "Um, what kind of meat's in there?" she asked, timidly.

Luckily the cook wasn't insulted. No doubt he thought she was asking for the recipe. "You take two pounds lean beef shank, half a calf heart, one set sweetbreads, salt and pepper, and my secret ingredient." He dipped the ladle into the bubbling stew and held it up for her to taste. "Louisiana hot sauce."

Abby took a sip. It was warm and spicy. "Whew!" she gasped. "That really is tasty!"

The cook grinned and put the lid back on the pot. "It'll clear your sinuses, I promise you." Then he wiped one hand on his apron and stuck it towards her. "My name's Silas Morehouse. I served with Captain Joe in the Union Army—we stood together at Antietam—and he invited me to come work at the Double Diamond."

Abby shook the cook's hand. "I'm Captain Joe's niece, Abigail."

Silas nodded gravely. "We're all mighty glad you're here. Mighty glad."

This caught Abby by surprise. "Really?"

"Oh my, yes." Silas pulled an apple out of a basket in the corner and tossed it to her. "It's hard on a ranchin' family that's got but one child. A ranch this size needs a big family to work it. That's why we're all so glad you're here. It'll be good to have another hard worker around the place."

Abby thanked Silas for the apple and wandered outside. His last words worried her.

Before Abby had left Iowa, Aunt Esther had mentioned something nasty about being shipped west to do hard labor. And on the train, many of the orphans had worried about the same thing.

Could this be true about her? Had the Carters brought her here just to be a ranch hand?

Abby suddenly felt the urge to run. Away from the ranch. And away from the Carters. She needed time to think.

Looking around, she spied the towering red rock cliff that sheltered the ranch on the north side and bolted toward it. She raced through the tall grass, until she reached the base of the bluff.

"This must be Box Canyon," she said out loud as she looked into a cleft in the rocks that led into a deep, narrow canyon. She'd heard her uncle talking about it on the long wagon ride to the ranch.

The rippling stream that bordered the pasture ran down the center of Box Canyon. To her right, an almost dry creek bed angled away from the stream, falling abruptly into a steep gully just below the cliff.

The entire field was covered in cornflowers and Indian paintbrush. Abby picked a bouquet of blue cornflowers, then made a place for herself in the tall grass. She closed her eyes and, tilting her head back, basked in the morning sun. One of her hands was pressed against the ground. And that's where she felt the rumbling.

It was tiny at first. Barely perceptible. But then it got bigger.

Abby's eyes popped open. Her arm was shaking. The rumbling grew louder, sounding more like thunder. Abby leapt to her feet. Her whole body was trembling.

"What's happening?" she cried out loud.

"Don't panic, Abby!" a girl's voice called from behind her.

It was Elizabeth.

Abby stumbled toward her cousin.

Elizabeth pulled Abby closer toward the cliff. "Stay close to the wall," she shouted over the thundering noise.

"But what's going on?" Abby pleaded, pressing her body against the rock wall. "What's that noise?"

Elizabeth pointed to the mouth of the canyon. "It's the wild horses!"

CHAPTER
FIVE

The Wild Mustangs

"Mustangs!"

Elizabeth's cry was drowned out by the herd of horses thundering out of the canyon.

"Oh, my gosh!" Abby gasped at the magnificent sight. There were white horses and roans, sorrels and bays. She even spied two pintos and a palomino. They raced around the pasture, tossing their manes and kicking out their back legs.

"There have to be at least twenty of 'em," Elizabeth shouted, keeping her body pressed flat against the base of the cliff. She pointed to the lead horse, a dappled grey stallion with white mane and tail. "Looks like the General has picked up a few more mares during this past winter."

The General, whose flanks and shoulders were covered with scars, galloped around the herd of mares and colts, gathering them together in a tight circle.

"Are these all yours?" Abby cried.

Elizabeth chuckled, stepping away from the cliff. "No! These mustangs are wild. They don't belong to anybody but themselves."

Abby watched as one horse—a dun-colored stallion with a black mane and black socks—danced away from the group. His nimble steps reminded Abby of the jig danced by performers in traveling minstrel shows. "Look at that one go!" she cried, clapping her hands. He looks like one of the buckdancers that used to come through Ames, Abby thought.

"He must be almost three years old," Elizabeth remarked. "Pretty soon the General is going to kick him out of the herd."

"Kick him out!" Abby gasped in dismay. "But why?"

Elizabeth shrugged. "There's usually only one stallion in the family band. There are a lot of mares, and some colts, but only one leader."

"But what will happen to him?" Abby asked,

watching the General nip at Buckdancer's flank to push him back toward the herd.

"He'll go find his own family. Sometimes a few of the young stallions get together and form a bachelor band. They travel around together, looking for their own mares."

"It must be fun to have a herd like this living on your ranch," Abby said.

Elizabeth grimaced. "Fun for them, maybe. But not for Papa. He can't stand the wild horses. Calls 'em broomtails."

Abby was shocked. "But how could Captain Joe not like them?"

"They eat the food our cattle need." Elizabeth pointed to the pasture in front of them. "Sometimes they even eat the apples off Mama's tree. For most of the year, we hardly ever see the Mustangs. Then in spring they come in from the canyons. They're usually half-starved from the long winter. But boy, are they tough! They've survived cougars, wolves, and freezing cold blizzards."

Abby looked at the Mustangs with even more admiration. These tough little fellows with their sleek coats and wild manes had to have some kind of fierce will to endure all of those hardships.

"Nobody takes care of them," Elizabeth continued.

"They take care of themselves."

Abby watched as Buckdancer continued to prance, both ears pricked forward and his mane flying in the wind. He looked so spirited and free. She tossed her own hair. "I wish I could be like them," she said, half to Elizabeth but mostly to herself.

"Really?" Elizabeth cocked her head. "But they're so wild."

Abby suddenly remembered the words of Budge Jenkins and her cousin, Lucas. "That girl's a wildcat. That's why they're shipping her off to the Wild West. It's the only place left that'll take her!"

That's right, Abby thought to herself. I am wild. I'm just like those Mustangs. I can take care of myself.

Secret Visits

A week later, Abby was hastily smoothing the quilt over her bed when Elizabeth stuck her head through the door.

"Mama wants to see you after you eat your breakfast," she announced.

"You don't have to yell at me," Abby snapped.

Elizabeth cocked her head. "I wasn't yelling, Abby. I was just delivering Mama's message."

Abby was feeling guilty about lazing in bed while everyone else did their morning chores. She was sure that Elizabeth resented her, and this made her grumpy.

Abby punched the pillow with her fist. "Tell Aunt Mary I'm hurrying as fast as I can."

Elizabeth nodded stiffly and left the room.

Abby wanted to run after Elizabeth and apologize for her behavior, but the little voice inside her stopped her. And instead of hurrying, Abby took a long time getting dressed.

A half hour later, Abby sauntered downstairs and paused at the bottom step. Carefully she leaned around the bannister and peered into the dining room. Usually the table was cleared, with only her table setting remaining. But today it was different. Her plate and silverware were gone.

Abby hurried toward the kitchen.

Aunt Mary was just finishing the morning dishes when Abby came in. She glanced over her shoulder and said, "Good morning, Abigail. There's a bowl of new potatoes on the table. Silas needs them peeled and delivered to the cookshack right away."

"What?" Abby was surprised. She was being told to work. Not asked. *Told.*

Aunt Mary picked up a towel and began drying the dishes. "Sourdough biscuits are in the breadbox. You can put honey or preserves on them, if you're hungry."

Aunt Mary was now telling her to get her own

breakfast! "I don't understand," Abby cried, putting her hands on her hips. "Did I do something wrong?"

Aunt Mary finished her dishes and hung the towel on the back of a kitchen chair to dry. "Of course not," she said as she picked up a broom and dustpan from the corner. "But Silas never waits breakfast. He only did that as a special favor while you were getting used to living here. But a week has passed."

"A whole week?" Abby said. It felt like she'd just arrived.

"We gave you that time to get settled in," Aunt Mary explained, as she swept the kitchen floor. "But now it's time for you to get on our schedule. Breakfast is at 6:30 sharp. After that, you're to help clear the dishes and wash up. Then you can get started on your job assignments."

"Job?" Abby repeated.

"Well, yes." Aunt Mary brushed the dirt into the dustpan and straightened up. "This is a working ranch. And every hand has to pull her own weight."

Abby felt her heart sink. She'd always had to do chores. At home, and when she was living with the Lloyds and her cousins. But this was different. This sounded like she was going to have to work for her keep.

It's just as I suspected, she thought, narrowing

her eyes at her aunt. They don't want another daughter. They want a servant.

Abby's tasks weren't difficult, but they took all morning to finish. Everyday as soon as she cleaned the breakfast dishes, she went straight to the cookshack to help Silas prepare for lunch. She hauled endless buckets of water from the pump to cisterns in the cookshack and bunkhouse. Then she helped in the barn, mucking out stalls and bringing hay down from the loft.

Elizabeth flew through her chores and often offered to help Abby with hers, but Abby always refused. If I can't do the work alone, she told herself, they'll ship me away.

For a whole week, Abby toiled away silently. In the hour or two after lunch, she'd slip off to the bluff, hoping to catch sight of the Mustangs.

On Monday, she finally saw them as they thundered down the canyon toward the open prairie. Unfortunately, the lead stallion spotted her. Before she could duck behind a rock, he had signaled the rest of the horses that it wasn't safe.

The General faced Abby, his head high and ears pricked forward, while the mares and colts left the pasture.

Abby froze.

The General snorted several times at her. It was as if he were saying, "You stay away from my family!"

"Don't worry, General," she whispered. "I won't do you any harm."

She watched as another horse paused at the mouth of the canyon. It was the young stallion with the black socks and black mane. She remembered him prancing in the pasture a few weeks before. He'd reminded her of a buckdancer from a traveling minstrel show.

The General turned. He took several steps toward the young stallion, then spun back, ready to face any surprise attack. Buckdancer mirrored the General's every move, tossing his head and snorting his own warning at Abby.

The two horses did it again, trotting toward the canyon and turning back abruptly.

Abby didn't move. She barely breathed.

Finally, at the mouth of the canyon, the General and Buckdancer reared up on their hind legs and slashed the air with their forelegs. Then they were gone.

Abby exhaled loudly at the impressive performance. Though she'd only seen the horses twice, she'd already noticed that they seemed to obey some strict rules.

The General always led the way into the pasture. First in line behind him was the palomino mare. Abby decided that she had to be the lead mare because whenever the General sounded the alarm, the palomino led the escape. And the other horses always followed in the exact order that they'd come in.

I guess they really are like a band, she thought with a smile. But instead of one that marches, this band gallops.

Abby the Outcast

W hen Abby returned to the ranch, she was surprised to see a covered wagon loaded down with supplies in front of the house. A team of draft mules had been unhitched and were standing calmly nearby as a redheaded girl looped feedbags over their heads.

A man and a woman sat chatting with Aunt Mary and Captain Joe on the front porch, while five children all under the age of ten raced around the wagon shrieking with laughter.

Elizabeth perched on the wagon, smiling at the little ones. When she spied Abby, Elizabeth sprang to her feet and raced to meet her.

"The Stoffards are here!" Elizabeth cried. "Isn't

47

that wonderful? They've got six kids and are so much fun."

"Are they neighbors?" Abby asked, watching the three littlest ones attempt cartwheels across the dirt road.

"You might say so. They live about fifty miles west of here. We hardly get to see them but twice a year. That's when they do their spring and fall supply run to Laramie." She gestured for the redheaded girl to join them. "This is Mabel Stoffard. She's twelve."

"Pleased to meet ya." Mabel stuck out her hand. Abby shook it, but didn't say anything. She was suddenly tongue-tied.

"Mabel's family is going to have supper with us," Elizabeth explained.

Abby tried to force a smile.

There was a thunk and then a cry from the vicinity of the wagon. Mabel looked over in dismay. "Eben's hurt himself, again. I had better go help."

As Mabel hurried to help her little brother, Elizabeth grabbed Abby's arm and pulled her toward the other children. "Come on and play. It'll be fun."

Abby dug her heels into the dirt. "I need to clean up first and finish the rest of my chores."

"Oh, pshaw!" Elizabeth waved one hand. "The chores can wait. We have guests!"

Abby didn't know what was making her so hesitant. Maybe the thought of meeting so many strangers at once. Or just that word—*guests.*

While she was at the Lloyds' or her Aunt Esther's house, *guests* meant that Abby wasn't wanted. She would be sent to sleep and eat in the shed to make room for them. It was a time when both houses made it clear that she was *not* considered part of their family.

"I'll go clean up and be right back," Abby said, anxious to get away.

Back in her room, Abby made an attempt to freshen up. Some weeds were caught in her tangled blonde hair, and she had a smudge of dirt on one cheek. She wiped the dirt from her face, but couldn't get her brush through the tangle in her hair. Finally she slammed the brush down on the dresser.

"It's no use," she told her reflection. "I don't belong with them. I'll just hide out in the barn until they leave."

Abby snuck out the back door and scurried along in the shadows of the sheds, until she reached the barn. She climbed the wooden ladder into the hayloft and hid in the far corner.

One of the barn cats had dropped a litter a few weeks before. A tiny black and white kitten wriggled its way into her lap, mewing loudly.

"What's the matter, little one?" she whispered to the kitten. "Did your mama go off and leave you all alone?" She stroked the top of the tiny cat's head. "I know just how you feel."

Suddenly the barn door swung open, and light poured onto the hay below. Abby kept perfectly still.

"Bet you can't catch me!" a boy bellowed as he raced into the barn. He was pursued by four other children.

It was the Stoffard kids.

"Let's jump out of the hayloft," the boy cried, charging for the ladder.

His younger brother, Eben, was right behind him. "Me first. It's my turn."

"No, it's my turn," the littlest girl cried. "Ain't that right, Mabel?"

Mabel stepped through the barn door and leaned against the wall, coughing. "Now, don't you kids quarrel," she rasped. "I don't feel so good. My throat burns, and I've got a headache."

"Why don't you sit over there?" Elizabeth pointed to a milking stool by the barn wall. "I'll fetch you a drink of water."

Mabel winced. "Water won't help, Elizabeth. It hurts to swallow."

By now, four of the Stoffard children had made it

into the loft. But luckily for Abby, they didn't notice her huddled in the corner.

The oldest boy, a redhead with freckles, called down to the floor below. "Say, what happened to that Abigail girl? I thought she was going to play with us."

"I'm not sure where she went," Elizabeth replied. "But she's a little, um, shy."

"Shy?" Mabel coughed. "Stuck up, more'n likely. She wouldn't even say boo to me. I bet she thinks she's too good to play with us."

"Now, Mabel, be fair," Elizabeth cut in. "I know Abby can be on the difficult side. I mean, we've all tried to break through the ice, but Mama says we have to remember Abby's an orphan. She lost her entire family a year ago."

"Then what's she doin' acting so uppity?" Mabel replied. "You'd think she'd be grateful you took her in."

Abby hung her head. It was humiliating to hear herself being talked about this way.

"I don't think Abby thinks of it like that," Elizabeth replied. "We are family, after all."

"Humph!" Mabel folded her arms and leaned back against the barn wall. "My ma said she has plenty of relatives, but no one will have her. If Captain Joe hadn't offered to take her in, she'd be stuck in the poorhouse, or in an orphan asylum."

Abby couldn't bear to hear another word. She set the kitten in the hay and crawled on her hands and knees toward a ladder on the wall. But as she neared the ladder, her foot knocked down a clump of hay.

"Who's there?" Elizabeth demanded, squinting up at the hayloft.

Abby leaned into the light. "It's me. Abigail."

Elizabeth's hand flew to her mouth. "Oh, Abby! Have you been there all the time?"

Abby didn't reply. She bolted down the ladder and out the rear door of the barn. Elizabeth was right behind her.

"Abby, stop, please!"

Elizabeth chased after Abby, catching up with her at the horse corral.

"Please Abby, let me talk to you," Elizabeth huffed, out of breath.

Abby was so upset, her face had turned a bright shade of purple. "I heard every word you and your snooty friend said," she cried.

"We didn't mean to hurt your feel—"

Abby wouldn't let Elizabeth finish. She was too angry. "You think I like being stranded on this dismal old ranch in the middle of nowhere with no friends?"

Elizabeth blinked in surprise. Finally she said,

stiffly, "If you made the least bit of effort to be nice, Abigail Armstrong, you'd make friends."

"Nice! Why should I be nice to a snob like Mabel?" Abby shot back.

Now it was Elizabeth's turn to get angry. "Mabel is *not* a snob," she said between gritted teeth. "You're the one who thinks you're better than everyone else. Lying in bed till all hours of the morning, acting shocked whenever you're asked to help out . . ."

"That was the first week," Abby protested. "I'm doing my work."

"And acting like it's killing you." Elizabeth spat her words at Abby. "You're slow as molasses with chores you don't like, and you have never once said a kind word to me."

"What?" Abby gasped.

Elizabeth's face was now as purple as Abby's. "We've all bent over backwards to be nice to you, but you don't deserve it." She put her hands on her hips. "You're rude, and unpleasant, and just plain mean."

Her words cut through Abby like a knife.

"Well, maybe I'll just leave!" Abby sputtered, fighting back tears.

"Go ahead," Elizabeth said. "See if I care!" With that she spun on her heel and marched back to the barn.

Abby turned and fled. Tears clouded her vision as she stumbled blindly away from the ranch.

Had she really been so hateful to all of them? The thought was almost too much to bear.

Behind her she could hear the *ding-a-ling-a-ling* of the cook's triangle, calling everyone to supper.

Abby hesitated for a fraction of a second. She knew she should go back, but how could she? Silas and Curly and even Big Tim must have been talking about her. She couldn't bear to face them or her aunt and uncle. Abby decided to keep running.

Her feet led her to the mouth of Box Canyon. She collapsed on her knees at the base of the bluff and buried her head in her hands.

No sooner had her knees hit the ground than she heard movement behind her.

Abby froze, straining to listen. She heard labored breathing.

She didn't dare look. What if it were a cougar, or a wolf? What would she do then? She squeezed her eyes closed, listening to her heart pound in her chest.

Another sound—the clatter of rocks! Abby's hands were now shaking. Whatever it was, it was going to get her. She knew it would!

Crrrack!

That sound was like a twig breaking. It was

followed by more rocks. But the sound wasn't coming any closer.

Should she look? Abby didn't know if she could. Every part of her was quivering. She had to!

Finally, Abby mustered every ounce of courage she had inside and slowly turned to look.

"Oh, my word!" she gasped in astonishment.

Buckdancer Is Hurt!

There, in the dried-up gully, six feet below Abby, was a Mustang. It was the young stallion with the dun-colored coat and black stockings, and he was hurt!

He limped in a circle around the creek bed, looking up at her. Each time he placed his weight on his left front leg, he reared his head back and snorted loudly.

Abby moved to the edge of the gully, and the Mustang skittered backwards. He whinnied shrilly.

He's trying to signal the General to come for him, Abby thought.

In the distance, she heard an answering whinny echo from the canyon, but no horse appeared.

He must have fallen and hurt himself, Abby thought, peering down.

This was the horse she'd seen dancing in the field so wild and free, like one of the buckdancers from the traveling minstrel shows. Now the Mustang looked dazed and confused. He limped frantically around the rocky creek bed, searching for a way to escape or a place to hide.

Abby inched toward the edge of the gully. "Don't worry, fella," she whispered. "I'm not going to hurt you."

The horse turned to face her, his sides heaving in and out like a blacksmith's bellows.

"Oh, my gosh!" Abby gasped, as she saw his wounds for the first time.

He had several gashes on his belly and a bleeding cut across his nose. A slash above his front knee oozed blood. The knee was so swollen he could barely put any weight on it.

Could a fall do this much damage? she wondered. Abby looked around the edge of the gully for the place where he must have fallen.

She found what she was looking for ten feet away at the base of a boulder.

The body of a bobcat lay bloodied and lifeless half-hidden by the tall weeds. The ground near the body was torn up in great big clods, and there was a gash in the edge of the gully where the Mustang must have fallen in.

"I'll bet you were battling this wildcat and the ground gave way beneath you, throwing you into this creek bed," she murmured.

The Mustang hobbled away from Abby. "You must be in such pain," she whispered. "Poor Buckdancer."

The horse's head flew up.

"Buckdancer," she repeated softly.

He didn't move, but continued to stare at her.

"Good Buckdancer," Abby cooed. "That's a good boy."

Abby knew if she went any closer, or made any sudden moves, the Mustang might panic and hurt himself even more. So she knelt at the edge of the gully, keeping her distance from him.

"It's all right," she murmured. "It's only me, little old Abby. I'd never think of hurting you."

Abby tried to keep her voice low and soothing. Buckdancer listened with his ears pricked forward.

"You're hurt, but you're going to get better," she told him. "You'll see."

She kept talking for nearly half an hour. Her back

and knees ached with the strain of sitting so still. She longed to shift her position, but she knew that might frighten the young stallion.

A melody came into her head. It was a song her mother used to sing to her when she was upset or hurt.

"Hush, little baby, don't say a word,
Mama's going to buy you a mockingbird.
If that mockingbird don't sing,
Mama's going to buy you a diamond ring . . ."

The more she sang, the more Buckdancer seemed to relax. His breathing eased and his nostrils no longer flared.

Abby studied his wounds carefully as she sang. She knew the gashes on his nose and belly would probably heal quickly. The blood was already scabbing over.

It was his leg that worried her. Was the knee swollen because of the wound above it? Or had he broken his leg in the fall? If it was a break, the Mustang was done for. He'd never be able to climb out of that gully.

In the week she'd been at the Double Diamond, she'd seen Waddy Hancock doctor a few horses. One horse had injured himself on the corral gate, giving himself a big gash on his shoulder. Waddy had been able to stitch up the gash in no time.

Another horse had strained a tendon. His leg had swollen up like Buckdancer's. Waddy had slathered the leg in plain old mud, explaining to Abby that the coolness of it would take down the swelling. Then later, Waddy covered the leg in a warm poultice he'd made out of bran.

"If I could just get back to the barn, maybe I could find some bandages and salve for your wounds," she whispered to the horse. "And I could grab a bucket and make up a bran poultice for your leg."

It was growing late. The sun was just about to set behind the bluff, and Abby knew she had better get back soon. Supper was long over, and the Carters would probably be coming to look for her.

She didn't want to leave the wounded Mustang, but she knew she had to.

"Water," she said to the horse, inching back from the edge of the gully. "You'll need water to help you through the night. And in the morning, I'll bring food."

She hurried toward the stream that ran out of Box Canyon into the pasture. "Now if I could just find something to put it in."

Abby was in luck. She found a wide metal pan sticking out of the weeds. It was covered with rust but seemed sound enough. Abby wondered if the pan

had been used by a prospector, then abandoned and left to rust when he headed north to Virginia City in the Territory of Montana.

Abby filled the pan as full as she could, then carefully carried it to the gully. It was only six feet to the bottom. If Buckdancer hadn't been wounded, he could have leapt that distance in a single bound. But it was hard for Abby to climb down while balancing a pan of water.

She decided to go the same route the Mustang had taken. Stepping gingerly over the body of the dead bobcat, Abby sat on her bottom and slowly slid down the side of the rocky creek bed.

Buckdancer backed as far away from her as he could limp.

"Stay calm, fella," she whispered, keeping her voice soothing. "I'm going to set this water here for you to drink. Then I'll be on my way."

She very carefully placed the pan between two rocks, so it wouldn't tip over.

"Here, boy," Abby called. "Here's some water. Come take a drink."

Then she scrambled up the side of the gully. The last thing Abby did before leaving was to move the body of the dead bobcat as far away from the gully as possible. She didn't want the smell of it to attract any other predators. Then she raced back to the edge of the gully.

"You take care of yourself, Buckdancer," Abby called softly. "Drink that water and keep out of sight. I'll be back for you in the morning."

Doctor Abigail

"**A**bigail!" Captain Joe boomed from the head of the breakfast table the next morning. "On this ranch, you let us know where you're going before you leave the premises."

His voice was as stern as his stony face.

Abby felt her cheeks instantly blaze pink.

Being lectured by Captain Joe was particularly embarrassing because the Stoffards had stayed overnight and had joined the family at the breakfast table.

Luckily Mabel wasn't there. She hadn't felt well and had asked if she could sleep late. But Elizabeth was sitting right across from Abby, glaring at her.

"This is still the Wild West," Captain Joe continued. "If anything ever happened to you in those canyons, we might never find you. Do you understand me?"

Abby nodded as she stared down at her plate of biscuits and sausage gravy.

"After we're done eating, help your Aunt Mary with the dishes and then get on over to the cookshack. Silas is preparing a big lunch basket for the Stoffards' trip home. Bring it back to the wagon."

"Yes, sir," Abby mumbled.

She had meant to tell Captain Joe or Waddy about Buckdancer, in the hope that they'd go help the injured horse. But something made her change her mind. The Captain appeared to be in a foul mood. And why would he help a "broomtail?" He'd probably shoot it.

Abby never looked up at the Stoffards. She ate her breakfast quickly and hurried off to help in the kitchen. The sooner she got through with her chores, the sooner she could get back to the cliff to help Buckdancer.

But things didn't work out the way she'd hoped.

After she hauled the picnic basket to the Stoffard's wagon, Aunt Mary caught hold of her arm. "Spring roundup starts in three days."

"What's that?" Abby asked.

"It's the time when we round up the cattle on the entire ranch, cut out the calves, and brand them."

"We have to do that?" Abby gasped.

"No, we don't," Aunt Mary chuckled. "But our cowboys do. We just go with them to the branding camp to help kick things off."

Abby frowned in confusion.

"Now don't look so downfaced, child." Aunt Mary swatted playfully at Abby's shoulder. "Roundup is about the most exciting event of the year in Medicine Bow. We like to celebrate it with plenty of food and lots of singing. It's sort of a going-away party for all the cowboys who'll be out rounding up our cattle."

"How many do they have to round up?" Abby asked.

"Last count we had over three thousand head of cattle."

Abby whistled softly between her teeth. Roundup would take a long time.

"We've got to start our baking now," Aunt Mary continued. "Silas is stocking supplies for the chuck wagon. Waddy and the boys are getting their tack and gear ready. And we're baking bread, biscuits, and pies to take along on the trail."

Abby's heart sank. She'd promised Buckdancer she'd be back that morning. Now it looked like she'd have to break her promise to the Mustang.

Abby made one more attempt to get back to the wounded horse that day. After supper, she helped with the dishes as usual, volunteering to dry so that she'd be the last person in the kitchen. But as she stepped out the back door, Abby bumped into Captain Joe smoking his pipe on the back porch.

"You're not planning to leave the grounds, are you?" he asked, eyeing the canvas bag tucked under her arm. She'd planned to use it to carry her supplies from the barn.

"No, Captain Joe. 'Course not."

He pointed to the sky with the stem of his pipe. "It's getting dark. And those clouds say it may rain. That's a dangerous time for anyone to be wandering around these canyons. You don't want to be caught in a flash flood."

Abby knew he was right, but her heart ached for the poor Mustang trapped in the gully.

"Now you go on back inside," Captain Joe said. "I hear Curly's offered to pick a few tunes for us on his guitar."

Reluctantly, Abby went back in the house.

That night she could barely sleep. She tossed and turned in her bed, while visions of the Mustang passed through her dreams. Around 3 A.M., she abruptly sat up, certain she'd heard Buckdancer whinny.

I don't care what Captain Joe says, she thought as she threw back the covers, I've got to help Buckdancer.

She touched her throat. It hurt. And her head ached. But she was bound and determined to get to that Mustang.

Abby felt in the darkness for her clothes. Then she dressed quietly, being careful not to wake Elizabeth. She carried her shoes in her hand and tiptoed downstairs. It was still pitch black outside, but she was able to find a lantern in the kitchen and light it.

Abby grabbed several apples from a bowl in the kitchen and stuffed some greens from the root cellar into her canvas bag.

She left the house and slowly made her way to the barn, terrified that she might trip on a bucket or step on a stick and wake the Captain or one of the ranch hands.

Abby filled the rest of the bag with bandages and other supplies that she'd found in the tack room. Then she grabbed a bucket that was near one of the troughs. The last thing she did was fill a flour sack with bran.

Abby hauled the lantern, heavy bucket, bandages, and bran across the open pasture, stopping at the stream for water. As she neared the canyon, the first rays of dawn were just lighting the eastern sky.

"Please be alive, Buckdancer, please!" she murmured over and over to herself. "Please be alive!"

Near the mouth of Box Canyon, Abby paused. She strained to hear some sign of life in the gully below. But all was quiet.

Not a whinny. Not even the barest rustle of movement.

She squeezed her eyes shut, afraid of what she might see, and inched forward. Her foot hit a rock and caused a pebble to slide down the side of the gully. And that's when she heard it. The smallest of sounds.

"Buckdancer, is that you?" Abby called softly.

She was answered by a feeble whinny.

Abby heard the clatter of rocks, as Buckdancer hobbled forward into the light.

"Oh!" she gasped. He was clearly much weaker than two days before. His knee was swollen to nearly twice its size.

Abby didn't hesitate. Holding tightly to the bucket and the canvas bag, she slid down the side of the gully on her bottom. The pan of water she'd placed between the rocks was bone dry.

"You must be thirsty," she said, as she set the bag

on the ground and slowly stood up with the bucket. "Abby's got a drink of cool water for you. Would you like that, fella?"

The wounded Mustang snorted his reply, but he didn't move.

Abby kept talking in a soothing voice as she inched forward. "I've got this bucket in my hand. It won't hurt you. I'm going to set it in front of you, so you can have a drink."

Buckdancer watched her warily as she approached. He even stumbled backwards a bit, but he didn't try to bolt.

"There you go." Abby lowered the bucket of water in front of him, and stepped back. "Go ahead, drink up. It's delicious."

Abby turned and walked slowly back to the canvas bag. Behind her she heard a few snorts, followed by loud slurping, as Buckdancer sucked in the much needed water.

"One down." Abby breathed a sigh of relief. "Now for the hard part. Tending that leg."

Abby pulled open the bag. Inside was a mason jar of hot water, some leaves of sneezewort, and a small jar of vegetable oil.

"Waddy told me that when a horse gets a sprain, the first thing you need to do is get the swelling down," she explained to Buckdancer. "I can't tell if your knee is sprained or not. My guess is the swelling has something to do with that gash above your knee. The poisons in your wound have probably drained into your knee. What we need to do is whip up a little bran paste so the swelling doesn't get any worse."

Buckdancer slurped at his water, raised his head, and listened. Then he drank again.

"You look like you really understand me," she said, with a smile.

Abby pulled the rusted tin pan out from between the rocks and placed it in front of her. She poured the bran and warm water in it and stirred them together with a stick. "I'm mixing this up, see?"

Buckdancer cocked his head alertly.

"Looks good enough to eat, doesn't it?" she said. "Add a touch of molasses, and you'd probably think you were in heaven."

Buckdancer hobbled two steps forward, throwing his head back each time his injured foot touched the ground.

"That must hurt like the dickens," she said, as she added the sneezewort leaves to the paste. "This sneezewort will help your wound heal. Waddy said the Indians taught him that."

She picked up the little jar of vegetable oil. "This

is to keep the bran moist. Otherwise it'll dry up and fall off your leg."

Abby dug in her bag for the greens and apples. "All right, boy, I've got a delicious treat for you. What do you say we make a deal? I'll give you these apples, and you'll let me smear this bran on your leg."

Buckdancer snorted and shook his head. She knew he was listening. But she had no idea if he would allow her to get anywhere near him, let alone his wound.

Slowly Abby stood up. She held an apple in front of her with one hand and the pan of bran in the other. As she inched her way towards Buckdancer, Abby sang the same soothing tune her mother had always sung.

"Hush little baby don't say a word,
Mama's gonna buy you a mockingbird."

The Mustang listened and watched as Abby drew nearer and nearer. But still he didn't try to move.

Now the apple was under Buckdancer's nose. He sniffed it curiously. Then, very delicately, he took it from Abby's fingers.

Abby smiled, but kept singing. The horse devoured the apple hungrily, so she handed him another. And another.

When Buckdancer had finished all of the apples,

Abby handed him a bunch of greens. He chomped those too. Bits of foam and apple spattered the sides of his mouth.

Still singing, Abby ever so carefully reached up to touch his neck. Her fingertips brushed the black mane and slid down firmly onto his thick yellow coat. Buckdancer kept chewing.

Abby's heart leapt up. It was hard to keep the excitement out of her voice. Buckdancer was actually letting her touch him!

She offered him some more greens, then slid her hand down his shoulder to his leg. Buckdancer stopped chewing and eyed her suspiciously.

Without dropping a note of her song, Abby scooped her hand into the pan to show him the bran poultice she'd made. He took a nibble of it, and Abby nearly laughed.

She changed the words of her song.

"This is a poultice that's good for you;
 It'll heal your leg and it's tasty, too."

The way she was finally able to smear the mixture on Buckdancer's wounded leg was to first offer him a bite, then smear a little on, then offer him another bite.

"A bite for you, and some for me;
 You'll feel good soon, just wait and see."

It seemed a miracle, but the wild horse let Abby cover his knee with the bran paste and then bandage it.

Abby worked as quickly as she could. Each passing second filled her with a fierce determination to make sure Buckdancer lived.

"I couldn't save my mama or papa," Abby whispered when she was done. "I couldn't save my baby brother. But, Buckdancer, I'm going to save you!"

Can't Stop the Roundup

"**O**w!" Abby yelped as she bent over to remove her shoes. Her head throbbed, and her throat burned so badly she could hardly swallow.

"What's the matter, Abby?" Aunt Mary asked, turning up the oil lamp in the front room. "Got a blister?"

It was Friday evening after supper, and Aunt Mary had asked Elizabeth and Abby to join her in front of the fire. The two girls hadn't spoken to each other in nearly a week, and sat as far away from each other as possible at meals.

"It's my head," Abby replied, rubbing her temples. "I have a terrible headache. And my throat hurts, too."

Elizabeth raised a skeptical eyebrow in Abby's direction. Right away, Abby knew what was in her cousin's mind.

Elizabeth thinks I'm pretending to be sick so I won't have to help on the spring roundup, she thought.

"But I'm fine," Abby added hastily, with a phony smile at Elizabeth.

Aunt Mary set the sock she had darned back in the basket beside her chair and looked from Elizabeth to Abby, and back again. "I'm not sure what's going on with you two," she declared as she picked up another sock. "But you're going to need to kiss and make-up before we leave tomorrow morning."

"Leave?" Abby repeated. "So soon?"

She heard a snort from Elizabeth.

"That's all we've been talking about," Aunt Mary said. "Why do you think we've been packing those food baskets and loading the wagons?"

Abby couldn't tell Aunt Mary that Buckdancer had been the only thing on her mind. For two days, she'd raced through her chores at lightning speed, just so she could spend time with Buckdancer.

Every day Abby carried fresh water and food to the gully. The second day she'd been thrilled to see that his swelling was actually going down. But

Buckdancer was still a long way from recovery.

"Everything's happened so fast," Abby said in a hoarse voice. "I didn't realize you were leaving tomorrow."

"You're going, too," Elizabeth said, folding her arms across her chest. "Isn't that right, Mama?"

Aunt Mary nodded. "We'll be off at first light. The branding camp is a ten mile ride away. We'll spend the night there and enjoy the celebration. Then we'll return Sunday evening."

Abby tried to swallow and winced in pain. "So we'll be gone for two days?" she rasped.

Aunt Mary nodded.

Abby frowned. That meant she wouldn't be able to get back to Buckdancer until Monday. He'd be without water and food for three whole days!

Aunt Mary patted Abby's hand. "Don't worry, Curly's staying behind to look after things. Soon as we get back, he'll join the boys at the branding camp."

"I'll stay with Curly," Abby said, leaping to her feet.

"Nonsense," Aunt Mary said, dropping her darning in her lap. "You're coming with us, child."

"But I could feed the chickens and collect the eggs," Abby said. "Curly can't take care of this whole ranch by himself."

"Abby is afraid she's going to have to work at the

branding camp," Elizabeth said to her mother.

"That's not true!" Abby shouted angrily at Elizabeth. The effort made her throat flare with pain, and she pressed her hand to her neck. "I'm always ready to work. That's why you brought me here, isn't it? To work for you?"

Aunt Mary looked shocked. "What are you talking about?"

"I do my chores," Abby continued. "I do the dishes, I help Silas in the cookshack, I clean the house. If that's not enough, than maybe you should find yourself another orphan. I hear there are plenty of them being shipped west. Whole trainloads."

"Abby!" Aunt Mary stood up, and the darning dropped to the floor. "That'll be quite enough!"

The room had begun to spin. Abby clutched the arm of the chair to keep her balance. "And if you need to ship me to the poorhouse, go ahead," she whispered. "Elizabeth won't miss me, I can tell you that."

Aunt Mary shot her daughter a sharp look. Elizabeth stared guiltily at her hands folded tightly in her lap.

"Abigail," Aunt Mary said evenly. "You're overtired. We all are. It's time for bed. You get some rest tonight, and things will look much better in the morning."

"You mean I can stay at the ranch?" Abby asked.

"Of course not," Aunt Mary replied sharply. "Now go to bed. I don't want to hear any more about it."

The room had stopped spinning, but Abby's head and throat still hurt. She stumbled off to bed, certain of only one thing. She absolutely, positively would not leave Buckdancer!

CHAPTER ELEVEN

Run Away and Hide!

"**O**nly a few yards more," Abby whispered to herself as she carefully felt the ground in front of her.

It was pitch black outside. The sun hadn't even thought about coming up yet. Still, Abby could hear sounds of life coming from the barn and bunkhouse as she tiptoed away from the ranch.

Her canvas bag was heavy. She'd stuffed it full of roots from the cellar and apples. She was also toting the flour sack full of bran and a jar of hot water.

"Whew!" Abby set the bag on the ground and took several deep breaths. A wave of dizziness made her stagger backwards. "I should have eaten breakfast."

Abby decided to kneel on the ground for a few seconds, until she could get her bearings. She felt miserable. Her throat was still raw, and the night before, while washing up before bed, she'd noticed a rash on her neck and chest.

"It's from worrying about leaving Buckdancer for so long," she'd told her reflection in the mirror.

Just before bed, she made up her mind not to go to the branding camp. Aunt Mary only needs me to serve food and clean up, she thought. But Buckdancer needs me to live.

Abby had slept in her clothes that night, so she could slip away before dawn.

Now she huddled on the ground, shivering, as the first rays of light peeked over Box Canyon.

"Brrr! Why is it so cold?" Abby said between chattering teeth. She felt her forehead with the back of her wrist. It was damp and clammy. "And why am I so sweaty?"

In the corral behind her the horses were snorting with excitement. "Curly and Big Tim are probably getting them ready to go," she murmured, looking nervously over her shoulder toward the ranch. "I'd better hurry, or someone'll see me crossing the pasture."

Abby rose to her feet and stood for a moment,

trying to steady herself. "Am I woozy," she said. "Must be from lack of sleep."

Clutching the flour sack and canvas bag close to her body, she hurried the rest of the way to the gully. Before she'd even neared the edge, she was greeted with a loud whinny.

"You know it's me, don't you, Buckdancer?" Abby asked as she peered over the ledge. "Are you telling me you're hungry? Is that what you're saying?"

Buckdancer hobbled forward a step. He wasn't exactly rushing to greet her, but at least he wasn't trying to hide. Abby took it as a good sign.

"How's your water?" Abby asked, checking the bucket she'd left with him. It was still half full. Then she dug in her bag for an apple and held it out to the Mustang.

Crunch! Buckdancer devoured the apple in one eager bite.

Abby swatted at her pinafore. "Where's your table manners?" she scolded with a chuckle. "You're getting slobber all over me."

She pulled another apple from the bag. The effort made her feel lightheaded. She took a deep breath and knelt in front of the Mustang. "While you chew on that, I'll take a quick look at your leg."

Abby was careful not to touch the horse unless it

was necessary. She didn't want him rearing up and kicking her. She leaned forward and peered at the leg. "The swelling has definitely gone down. But I think we need to do something about that wound."

The gash above the leg still oozed a milky fluid. Abby was afraid it might be getting infected.

She pulled the canvas bag toward her and took out all of her supplies. At the bottom, in a little tin, she'd packed some dried marigold leaves.

"My mama believed that pot marigold was good for just about everything. Anytime any of us ever cut ourselves, she rubbed marigold leaves on the wound. And it really did heal faster."

Buckdancer had finished chewing and was watching her, his ears pricked forward.

Also in the bottom of the bag, carefully wrapped in cloth, were Abby's treasures. She removed the little gold necklace and held it up for Buckdancer to see.

"This belonged to my mama. It's all I have left of her. I'm not sure why there's only half a heart on this chain," she said, her eyes welling with tears. "But that's how my heart feels. Broken clear in two."

While she was putting the locket away, Buckdancer leaned forward, snorting warm breath onto the top of her head. She felt his soft muzzle nibble on her hair.

"My hair may look like hay," she said with a giggle, gently touching the horse's velvety nose. "But I promise you it's just hair."

She unscrewed the lid on the hot water jar and poured some water into the tin pan, along with the bran and the marigold leaves. While she mixed the poultice, Buckdancer nibbled on the edge of the canvas bag, knocking it over.

The tintype of Abby's father fell onto the ground. As she picked it up, a sudden chill made her shiver. "Brrrr. I don't know how it's possible for it to be so cold out here and me sweating so." She put her hand to her moist forehead. "But I am."

Buckdancer snorted in response.

Abby held the picture up for the horse to see. "This is my papa. He was a newspaper man. Very smart. He liked to read and write stories about the Wild West. But I know he would never have been comfortable living here."

The poultice was ready. Abby carefully placed the picture back in her bag and began to apply the sticky paste to Buckdancer's knee.

"Papa liked houses and towns and people." Abby slowly worked the bran mixture up onto Buckdancer's wound. "Mama was the same. She loved entertaining in her parlor. She even had a ladies' book club. They would read books about, well, most anything, then all get together to talk about them."

Buckdancer flinched, jerking backwards.

"Easy boy," Abby cooed. "I know this hurts, but it's good for you. So you're just going to have to trust me."

Somehow Buckdancer understood her words, because he didn't move again until she was finished applying the poultice.

Abby rinsed her hands in the leftover water from the jar and began putting her things back in the bag. As she was rewrapping the tintype, two blue ribbons fell into her lap.

"Oh, Buckdancer!" Abby pressed the ribbons to her cheek. "I showed you all of my other treasures, but I didn't show you these. They belonged to my brother Ben. He was just a baby, barely a year old, when he—he got sick."

She held up the ribbons, letting them flutter in the breeze. We tied his booties with these. Ben was always pulling at them, untying 'em. He just didn't like shoes. Liked to be free to wiggle his toes."

Buckdancer ducked his head under the ribbons. For a moment they fluttered against his mane.

Abby stroked his neck and he didn't pull away. She picked up several strands of his hair and in a moment of inspiration, carefully braided one of the ribbons into his mane.

"There!" she exclaimed. "You look better already."

As if in reply Buckdancer tossed his mane, letting loose with a loud whinny.

He was answered by a fierce gust of wind that whistled down the canyon.

Abby wrapped her arms around herself, shivering. She glanced nervously at the sky. "Dawn's broken, but dark clouds are moving in. Looks like bad weather is on the way."

She bent over to pick up her canvas bag and completely lost her balance. She fell heavily onto her knees.

"I don't feel well," she groaned. "My head is going round and round."

Thunder rumbled ominously in the distance. Buckdancer hobbled back toward the side of the gully, his head jerking back with each step on his lame leg.

Abby lifted her head to look at him, but her vision was blurred. "It's gonna be a bad storm, isn't it?" She shut her eyes.

Buckdancer whinnied again.

Abby forced herself to her feet as a bolt of lightning zigzagged across the sky and, less than a second later, thunder boomed just above them.

Abby clutched her stomach. Her insides were cramping. Her throat burned. She tried to take deep breaths of air through her nose.

She turned and faced the ranch as the sky erupted in thunder and lightning.

"Gotta get back," she rasped, stumbling blindly across the pasture.

Halfway to the ranch, Abby again felt terribly dizzy. The horizon started to spin. Abby reached out with one hand to steady herself.

Lightning lit up the darkening sky.

Then her knees buckled under her. "I'm not going to make it," she gasped.

And everything went black.

The Fever

Abby's eyes fluttered open.

I'm in a room, she thought. Is that Aunt Mary?

A blurry face bent over her, and a hand smoothed her damp hair back from her forehead. A cool cloth was pressed across her eyes.

Mmm, that feels good, she thought.

Abby started to drift off again. Back into that misty world of the past. She was riding her pony, Toby, trotting in a wide circle around her mother. Little Ben was laughing and laughing. Then he faded from view.

Hot. I feel hot, Abby thought. She moaned. Sweat dripped down her neck.

"Curly found her in the pasture," a deep voice spoke from across the room, "halfway to Box Canyon."

Captain Joe? Abby turned her head.

"She was burning up, and half out of her mind, muttering something about a horse."

Buckdancer? Abby wanted to sit up, but she couldn't get her body to move. Everything hurt.

"When Mary found her missing," Captain Joe explained, "we put a hold on the roundup."

"I was so worried." Aunt Mary's voice shook with emotion. "Afraid she'd run off. A child that young, with no experience, wouldn't last two days in the wild."

The cloth was lifted from Abby's eyes. A strange man bent his face near hers. He wore wire-rimmed glasses and smelled of camphor. "Her body is covered in the rash. And see that pale area around the mouth? It's one of the sure signs. That, and the raspberry tongue."

The man tugged at Abby's jaw, pulling her mouth open. "See how her tongue is swollen and bright red?"

Abby swatted feebly at the face swirling in front of her. Don't know you, she thought. Go away!

"The child's got the fever, all right," the doctor

announced, stepping away from the bed. "Heard there's been a bad outbreak of it all around Laramie."

"The Stoffards were just over at Laramie," Captain Joe rumbled. "And their daughter Mabel was feeling pretty poorly."

"It's the children that suffer the most," the doctor said solemnly. "Whatever you do, keep Elizabeth away from Abby. Scarlet fever is highly contagious."

Scarlet fever? Abby raised her head and croaked, "No. Please, no!"

Someone rushed forward and placed another cool cloth on her head. "There, there, honey. Aunt Mary's here. You're going to be all right."

"I didn't think she could hear us, Doctor," Captain Joe whispered.

"She hears, all right," the doctor whispered back. "But her mind is confused. The fever's made her delirious."

"Buckdancer!" Abby wailed, throwing the wet cloth off her head. "Have to help Buckdancer. He's hurt!"

"Who is this Buckdancer?" the doctor asked.

"I don't know," Captain Joe replied. "Never heard of him."

Abby batted at the sheet covering her body. She had to get to Buckdancer!

"Doctor? What can you do about the fever?" Aunt Mary asked quietly.

"Maybe we had best step outside to talk about it."

The blurred shapes left the room. Abby was alone.

Images of Buckdancer, hurt and bleeding, swirled through her brain. They were followed by thoughts of the bobcat, alive and attacking. Abby thrashed her head back and forth on her pillow.

Suddenly she heard a whinny.

"Buckdancer?" Abby murmured, barely able to raise her head. "Is that you?"

Abby was certain the wounded horse was calling her.

"Have to go to him," she mumbled, throwing back the sheet. She flung herself out of the bed and hit the floor with a thud. But Abby didn't feel a thing. All she could think about was Buckdancer. He needed her.

Abby blinked, trying to make the room swim into focus. She found the door and crawled toward it. Her nightgown was soaked with sweat, and her arms were weak, but still she crawled forward.

When she finally reached the door, she pulled it open, then fell into the hall. She lay helpless, her cheek pressed against the wood floor. "Help," she mumbled. "Have to get help."

Elizabeth was standing at the far end of the hall. "Abigail!" she cried. "What are you doing out of bed?"

Abby was able to muster enough strength to lift her head. "Elizabeth, help me. Please."

Elizabeth pressed a handkerchief to her mouth and backed away. "Oh, Abby, I'd like to," she cried, "but I'm not supposed to go near you."

"It's not me," Abby moaned. "It's Buckdancer. His leg is hurt."

Elizabeth leaned forward. "Is Buckdancer a horse?"

"Yes!" The room began to swirl again.

"He's at the bluff," Abby gasped. Then her eyes rolled back in her head, and she collapsed.

Abby on the Mend

The room was bathed in sunlight. Abby had no idea how long she'd been lying in bed, but suddenly she felt hungry. Very hungry!

Abby pulled herself to a sitting position and looked around. She pressed her hand to her forehead. It was cool. Finally!

She checked the back of her hands. "No more spots," Abby whispered.

Abby was about to throw back the covers and leap out of bed when she noticed a woman asleep in the chair opposite her.

"Aunt Mary," Abby said gently.

Her aunt was wearing the same green dress she'd

been wearing when the doctor had first appeared. Her hair, which was always drawn into a neat bun at her neck, was mussed. Long blonde strands fell across her drawn and tired face.

Suddenly Aunt Mary's eyes opened. She stared at Abby for several seconds. Then her face blossomed into a huge smile.

"You're better, Abby," she declared. "I can see it from here."

Aunt Mary sprang to her feet and ran to the bedroom door. "Joe! Elizabeth! Come quick!"

Abby heard footsteps pound down the hall. Then the door was thrown open. It was Elizabeth.

"Thank heavens!" she gasped, clapping her hands together. The relief on Elizabeth's face was genuine.

Captain Joe appeared behind Elizabeth, resting his hands on her shoulders. He took one look at Abby and shook his head in wonder. "I do believe we've had a miracle."

Then he and Aunt Mary rushed over and smothered Abby in hugs. "I am so happy!" Aunt Mary said as she smoothed Abby's hair off her forehead, straightened her nightgown, and squeezed her again and again. "Oh, dear child, I can't tell you how happy I am."

"Silas!" Elizabeth shouted down the hall. "Quit

dishing up breakfast and come here!"

Then she ran to the window and yelled for the ranch hands. "Hey, Curly! Everybody! Abby's well. Come see!"

Abby smiled. Maybe everyone really does care about me, she thought. The attention felt good, but she itched to question Elizabeth about Buckdancer.

Elizabeth joined her parents at the side of the bed. "We were all so worried about you," she said, clutching Abby's hand. "Curly and Big Tim have been stopping by every morning and every night. And Silas keeps whipping up new batches of Anything'll-Do broth, hoping you'll be well enough to eat it."

The weather-beaten shape of Big Tim suddenly appeared at the open window. "Well, I'll be hogtied," Big Tim declared, his eyes glittering with pleasure. "If it ain't our Miss Abby, come back to join us."

Abby smiled and waved. "Howdy, Big Tim! Have I been gone long?"

Big Tim tipped his hat back on his head. "Too long, if you ask me. By my recollection, it's been nearly a week since we were supposed to leave for round-up."

"A week!" Abby's smile slid off her face. "Oh, no!"

"What's the matter?" Aunt Mary asked.

Abby turned to Elizabeth. "Buckdancer . . . Is he . . . ?"

A sly smile crept across Elizabeth's lips.

"What?" Abby demanded. "What is it?"

Elizabeth wiggled her eyebrows at Big Tim and then said in a very mysterious voice. "We have a little surprise for you, Abby."

Abby opened her mouth to speak, but Elizabeth raised a firm hand. "Not another word. Just do as I say."

While Big Tim turned and whistled for Curly, Elizabeth tied a bandanna around Abby's eyes.

"All right, Papa," Elizabeth announced. "She's ready."

Captain Joe scooped Abby up in his arms and carried her down the hall, through the dining room, and out the back door.

When she heard the *crunch, crunch* of Captain Joe's boots on gravel, Abby knew they were crossing the ranch yard. Soon they were joined by more footsteps and jingling spurs, as their group got bigger.

When they'd covered quite a distance, Elizabeth barked in her best imitation of her father's military voice. "Company—halt!"

Everyone stopped walking at once.

Abby was still in Captain Joe's arms when Elizabeth removed the blindfold. Elizabeth stepped back and cried, "Look!"

There in the corral, with his head held high and his dark mane blowing in the wind, was Abby's magnificent Mustang.

"Buckdancer!" she cried.

The Mustang wheeled to face them, his nostrils flaring.

"Captain Joe, would you set me down, please?" Abby asked.

He grinned and nodded. The second her feet touched the ground, Abby ducked under the railing into the corral.

"Careful," Big Tim warned. "He may be limping, but he's still a wild one."

"Don't worry," Abby replied, steadying herself against the rail. "Buckdancer knows me. Don't ya, fella?"

When the Mustang saw her, his ears pricked forward, and he whinnied loudly.

"Son-of-a-gun," Curly announced from his perch on the corral gate. "He *does* know you."

As if to prove the cowboy's words, Buckdancer took three steps toward Abby.

"You're still limping," she said, eyeing his wounds. "But that gash is almost healed, and your knee looks much better."

"Somebody did one nice job of doctorin' that

horse," Waddy Hancock remarked, leaning against the fence rail. "Course, whoever it was had to go and use a whole mess of bran from our barn to do it . . ."

"Ah, Waddy, don't be such a skinflint," Big Tim said, swatting good-naturedly at the foreman with his hat.

"Yeah, Waddy," Silas cut in. "I believe my supply of apples and greens suffered more damage than your horse feed."

Abby smiled guiltily over her shoulder at the cook. "Sorry, Silas. But I had to do it."

"I understand," Silas said, nodding solemnly. "And just to show you what a generous soul I am, I've brought your fine Buckdancer some breakfast."

Silas dug into the pocket of his apron and handed Abby a bunch of greens and two shiny red apples.

Abby could barely see to take the food because of the tears in her eyes. "Thank you, Silas."

She turned to look at Waddy, Big Tim, and Curly. Then at Elizabeth and her aunt and uncle. "Thank you all for saving me. And Buckdancer."

She held an apple out in front of her, and Buckdancer limped forward. He sniffed the apple, then worked his way up her hand, and nibbled at the lace on the base of her sleeve.

Abby giggled softly. "Yep, it's me. I bet you thought I was never coming back."

Two Hearts Are One

The next day, Elizabeth and Abby sat side by side on the back porch peeling potatoes and watching Buckdancer. Abby had recovered enough to sit outside, but she still wasn't strong enough to run around the ranch.

"He sure is handsome," Elizabeth remarked as she dropped her peeled potato into the tin pot that sat between them. "And full of spirit."

"And strong," Abby added, as Buckdancer circled the corral. "Why, look at him. He's hardly limping any more."

Buckdancer turned to look at the girls as if he'd heard them.

"You know we're talking about you, don't you?" Abby said.

Buckdancer answered her with a defiant toss of his head and a loud snort.

"I love the way his mane flies in the breeze," Abby said, watching him circle the corral once more.

"Mane?" Elizabeth repeated. "Oh! I almost forgot." She dug into the pocket of her pinafore and produced a single blue satin ribbon. "Curly said this was tangled in Buckdancer's mane when they brought him up from the gully. Couldn't figure how it got there."

Abby set her potato and knife back in her bowl and wiped her hands clean. Then she gently took the ribbon from Elizabeth. "That belonged to my brother, Ben. It was the tie for one of his booties."

Elizabeth studied Abby's face intently. "I guessed you must have braided it into Buckdancer's mane," she said in a quiet voice.

Abby nodded. "I wanted to give him something special to help him get better."

Elizabeth set her bowl on the chair beside her and went into the house. When she returned, she was carrying Abby's canvas bag. "Curly also found this near Buckdancer. He gave it to me to keep for you."

Abby hadn't really shared any information about

her past with Elizabeth. She decided it was about time she did.

"When my family . . . passed on," she began quietly, "I wanted to keep something to remember them by. The Lloyds took almost everything we had, but I managed to save these."

Abby held up her treasures. First, the tintype of her father. "This was my papa. Your Uncle Will."

As Elizabeth carefully held the fragile glass, tears welled up in her eyes. "He's very handsome. You must miss him terribly."

Abby nodded. "So much, I ache inside."

Then she held up the other ribbon to Ben's booties. And lastly she presented the gold necklace with the broken heart.

Elizabeth took one look at it and let out a startled cry. "Oh! You have to show this to Mama!"

Aunt Mary heard the commotion on the porch and came running out to see what was the matter. Elizabeth's jaw was moving up and down, but no words were coming out.

Aunt Mary took one look at the heart, gasped, and disappeared into the house.

"Elizabeth! What's going on?" Abby asked.

Aunt Mary quickly returned, cradling an identical gold necklace in her hand. She held up the broken heart pendant. "Your mother gave this to me when Joe and I went west."

Aunt Mary was so full of emotion she could barely speak. "She always said that we were two hearts that beat as one, and that as long as we were apart, she would feel that she only had half a heart."

Aunt Mary held out her half of the heart with a shaky hand and pressed it against Abby's half. The two pieces snapped together perfectly.

"Do you see, sister?" Aunt Mary called up to the heavens. "Our hearts are finally reunited."

When Aunt Mary pressed her heart against Abby's, something inside Abby clicked. It was as if her own heart were no longer broken.

When Aunt Mary turned to Abby and opened her arms, Abby fell right into them. "This is a very big day for many reasons," Aunt Mary said. "Captain Joe made a decision last night."

"What, Mama?" Elizabeth asked, eagerly.

"He talked to Waddy and the boys, and he's decided that you can keep Buckdancer for your own horse, Abby."

"My own?" Abby gasped.

Aunt Mary nodded, happily. "Everyone on a ranch has a horse. And Buckdancer will be yours. Curly said he would help break him after Buckdancer's knee has healed."

Abby's brow was suddenly creased with a frown. "Break Buckdancer? I could never allow that."

Elizabeth touched Abby's arm. "*Break* is just an expression. It means Curly will work with him until he's no longer wild. Then he'll saddle him up so you can ride him."

Abby tried to imagine Buckdancer with a saddle on his back and a bit in his mouth, chewing oats from a bucket. She hated the thought.

"Buckdancer is a wild horse," she said firmly, watching him circle the corral once more. "He deserves to run free."

Buckdancer finished her statement with a shrill whinny.

"See," Abby giggled, "he's just itching to break loose."

"It's your decision," Aunt Mary said, touching the

gold heart once more. She quickly dabbed at her eyes with a handkerchief, then cleared her throat.

"You girls get to work now and finish those potatoes. In the meantime I'll talk to Joe. And as soon as he and Waddy think that Mustang's well enough, we'll take Buckdancer home."

Abby nodded. "Back to Box Canyon."

Finally Home

The sun was just peeking over the top of the red cliffs when Abby and Elizabeth arrived at Box Canyon.

Abby had planned to release Buckdancer by herself. Then she realized this was a very special moment and ought to be shared with a special friend.

"Giddyup, Baldy," Abby clucked to the big bay she was riding. By now she was well on her way to becoming a regular ranch girl, and Big Tim's horse had become one of her favorites.

Elizabeth rode beside her on her palomino, Sugarfoot. Buckdancer followed along behind them.

Abby turned in her saddle to look at the Mustang. "Buckdancer knows something's up. Look at the way that he prances behind Sugarfoot."

Elizabeth chuckled, as the horse skittered sideways with excitement. "To watch him dance, you'd never guess he was ever lame."

Abby nodded. "Waddy and Curly took good care of him. Two weeks of food from the barn and he's practically back to new."

Elizabeth smiled at Abby. "Same goes for you. You look better than ever. Tanned, not so scrawny. Why, even your hair looks good."

"I combed and braided it." Abby turned her head sideways to display the braid that stretched to the center of her back. "It's about time, huh?"

The girls had reached the opening to Box Canyon, but neither one wanted to dismount. It was Buckdancer who gave them the signal.

He let loose with a shrill whinny that echoed around the canyon walls.

"Okay, I get the message," Abby said, hopping nimbly off Baldy's back. She walked back to Sugarfoot and untied Buckdancer's rope. "Just give me a second here, and you can be on your way."

Abby coiled the rope up till she reached Buckdancer's nose. Then she dug into her pocket for the apples Silas had slipped her that morning at breakfast. "I'm going to miss you," she murmured as she slipped the halter off his head. "But I'll be watching for you. From right over there." Abby pointed to the base of the cliff. "And every spring when you come tearing out of that canyon, I expect you to at least give a nod in my direction. Is that understood?"

Buckdancer didn't respond. His ears were cocked forward, listening.

Elizabeth, who was still in the saddle on Sugarfoot, holding Baldy's reins, called, "Abby, do you feel it? That rumbling?"

Abby nodded. It felt like an earthquake beneath her feet.

"Better get Baldy and Sugarfoot out of here," Elizabeth cried. "Before it's too late."

Abby leapt onto Baldy's back and gave him a nudge to get going. "Hi yaw!"

The girls galloped away from Buckdancer as the rumbling grew louder and louder. Suddenly a sound like rolling thunder filled the air.

Buckdancer whinnied loudly.

He was answered by another whinny.

"Whoa, fella!" Abby reined Baldy to a halt.

Buckdancer reared up and batted the air with his forelegs just as the herd of Mustangs burst out of the mouth of the canyon.

The General was in the lead, followed by the palomino mare. They led the herd in a wide circle around Buckdancer. The General snorted a loud greeting, and Buckdancer took his place in the band.

Abby wiped the tears from the corners of her eyes as she watched.

Elizabeth rode back to join her. "It's hard to let him go, isn't it?"

"I thought Buckdancer was an orphan like me," Abby said, fighting hard to keep her chin from quivering. "But I was wrong. That's his family. The entire band of wild horses."

"And here is your family." Elizabeth reached out and took hold of Abby's hand. "Right here on the Double Diamond Ranch."

Abby squeezed her cousin's hand. Then the two girls watched as the band of wild horses pounded back toward the canyon.

At the gap in the cliff, Buckdancer separated himself from the others for the briefest moment. He paused, looking back at Abby.

She raised her hand in farewell.

When Buckdancer had completely disappeared from view, Abby turned to Elizabeth and smiled through her tears.

"Come on, Elizabeth. Let's go home."

FACTS
ABOUT THE BREED

You probably know a lot about Mustangs from reading this book. Here are some more interesting facts about this feisty American horse.

∩ Mustangs generally stand between 13.2 and 15 hands high. Instead of using feet and inches, all horses are measured in hands and inches. A hand is equal to four inches.

∩ Mustangs come in all colors. Often, like many horses of Spanish origin, they have an eel, or dorsal stripe, a dark stripe that runs from the withers along the spine to the top of the tail. Common colors among Mustangs include roan, dun, and buckskin.

∩ Although the conformation, or build, varies from horse to horse, Mustangs generally have small, sturdy bodies with short, strong legs and hard hooves. Their hooves are so hard that they can travel over rough ground without injury and without wearing shoes.

∩ The name Mustang comes from the Spanish word meaning group or herd of horses.

∩ Mustangs are descended from the horses that were first brought to Mexico by Spanish settlers in the sixteenth century. By the seventeenth century, the Spaniards had begun to breed their horses near present-day Santa Fe, New Mexico. Some of these horses ran away and became feral, or wild. These feral herds then moved north into the western plains of the United States.

∩ When cattle ranching took hold in the United States in the nineteenth century, large numbers of Mustangs became cow ponies. Cowboys caught and trained Mustangs to perform a variety of jobs. Mustangs learned to cut, or separate, a single cow from the herd. They served as roping horses and as "night horses." Night horses must be especially sure footed and able to see well in the dark.

∩ Many of the Native American tribes also caught and tamed Mustangs. These horses became an important part of life on the Plains. Horses enabled Native American tribes to hunt large number of buffalo and to make the seasonal moves of the village more easily.

∩ Members of the Nez Percé tribe, who were known as excellent horsemen, developed the Appaloosa breed from feral Mustangs.

∩ Occasionally an Arabian or Thoroughbred imported to the New World from Europe ran away from home and joined a Mustang herd.

∩ In 1900, approximately one million wild Mustangs roamed the western United States.

∩ Over the years, many Mustangs have been captured and tamed. Others met less happy fates. Before the passage of a law to protect them, Mustangs in the western United States were rounded up by helicopter, killed, and turned into dog food.

∩ In 1971, the Wild Free Roaming Horse and Burro Act was passed. This law protects Mustangs from being rounded up and killed. The Bureau of Land Management, an agency of the United States Federal Government, is responsible for the well being of these feral horses.

∩ Today there are approximately 35,000 wild horses in the western states. They roam mostly in Nevada and Wyoming. When necessary, the Bureau of Land Management rounds up the horses and puts some of them up for adoption. In this way they keep the wild horse population from becoming too large for the limited amount of grassland available to them.

∩ Since older horses are harder to tame, Mustangs put up for adoption are less than five years old. Even so, of the 130,000 horses adopted under this program, 13,000 of them have been returned to the Bureau of Land Management because they were too difficult to keep.

∩ Today there are a number of organizations that exist to protect wild Mustangs. They include: the International Society for the Protection of Mustangs & Burros of Scottsdale, Arizona; the National Mustang Association of Newcastle, Utah; and the American Feral Horse Association of Boise, Idaho.

Ω In addition, several breed registries, like the North American Mustang Association & Registry of Mesquite, Texas, help to preserve the Mustang's genetic heritage by encouraging registration and good breeding practices among domesticated Mustangs.